Jesse Gra

in

HIT THE GROUND RUNNING

To William!
I love you,
little man!
Stay Wild!

BY JESTON TEXEIRA

Printed in the United States of America

Edited by Adrian Gazaway

First Printing, 2018

ISBN-13: 978-1721691432
ISBN-10: 172169143X

They will fight against you,
But they shall not prevail against you.
For I am with you," says the Lord, "to deliver you."

-Jeremiah 1:19 (NKJV)

Chapter One

Jesse Granger wasn't like other boys. Most boys were born in a hospital, but Jesse was born in the wild. Most boys went to school, but Jesse's parents taught him from home. Most kids played with other kids, but Jesse played with lion cubs and baby elephants. Sometimes he got lonely and wished he was like other kids. He was lucky, though. Most kids have never been chased by playful monkeys or ridden an elephant with their parents. Jesse Granger wasn't like most boys. But that was fine by him.

** **

Before Jesse was born, his parents were in a rainforest searching for the rare Teyano tree frog that was rumored to be extinct. It had been over twenty years since its last official sighting. Natives to the land believed the tree frog held power over life and death and that its secretions contained magical healing powers. A lot of people sought the frog to cure their ailments. Those who wished to exploit the frogs' properties for profit hunted down and killed almost all living specimens. Jesse's parents didn't want to hurt the frog, though. Or use its secretions to run tests. Their life's work consisted of studying, protecting, and preserving the lives of endangered animals no matter how small. They held out hope that man hadn't hunted these little guys to extinction.

"Come on!" Mrs. Granger called out. "I think I've spotted one!"

Mr. Granger ran over to his wife but

the frog took off. The couple wasn't able to get a good look at the frog before it leapt into the brush. They were both certain it was the elusive Teyano tree frog, though.

"So close!"

Their careers would be defined by their next steps. They could follow that frog into the lush rainforest, track him down, and capture him like those that came before them. Or they could let him be free. They could go on being content with the hope that somewhere among the trees, this incredible tree frog was thriving. They chose the latter with no need for discussion. Not long after their monumental discovery, Mrs. Granger's round belly got a sharp pain. She cried out to her husband, "It's time!"

A few of the natives aiding the expedition rushed to her side and assisted Mrs. Granger in delivering her new baby boy. He cried loudly into the night sky. His mother held him close and comforted him. But something was wrong. The boy was sick. His skin was pale and it was clear that his lungs weren't working like they should have been. He took short, ragged breaths and had a raspy cough. Symptoms of a lung disease that ran in Mr. Granger's family. He could feel it. It pained his heart that the disease had been passed on to his child. But this was no time for mourning. It was time for action. His boy's life depended on it. But Mr. Granger was at a loss.

"What are we going to do?" he cried.

"I don't know," Mrs. Granger whispered. She looked up at the night stars and made a wish. She sent her hopes and fears out to God, the Universe, whoever would listen. *Save my son,* she thought, with longing in her heart and tears falling down her face. She would give anything for her little boy to be safe and sound.

The parents needed to get their son to a hospital, but it's not easy to get medical help in the middle of a rainforest. As the boy's condition worsened and the Grangers began to lose hope, a tree frog appeared. A Teyano tree frog. More of the small creatures followed and approached the sick newborn. They hopped onto his arms, legs, and forehead and began to croak. A low hum filled the air. As the Grangers wiped

tears from their eyes, their son's skin gained a rosy pink color and his breathing became normal. With their work finished, the frogs disappeared back into the trees.

"It's a miracle," Mrs. Granger declared.

Mr. Granger kissed his wife, and held their newborn baby. "We'll name you Jesse," he said.

Jesse was healed. Though they never believed in the myths before, the Grangers did now. There was no denying that something truly magical had just taken place. Mr. Granger was eternally grateful. He held his new little family close and knew, in that moment, that he would raise Jesse to care for wildlife as he and his wife did. It was nature that helped save his son. The least he could do was show it the same love and respect.

** **

8 YEARS LATER

Jesse ran around the park. Animals

that may have otherwise died in the wild lounged in the sunny weather. It was a big day for the Grangers. The day after Jesse was miraculously healed, his parents decided to return the favor to nature. They went home and worked for years to build a wildlife refuge where they could not only preserve wildlife, but educate the public on it as well. After all that work and planning, it finally came time for Granger Park to celebrate its grand opening. Though they had no proof that the frog truly did save Jesse, the Grangers knew in their hearts it did and often shared that story with others. Today was one of those days where they shared that special story.

A group of children came to visit the Granger Park as part of their studies. Mrs. Granger called out for Jesse to join her and his father at the podium. The local newsmen had arrived to document this special day. It wasn't often that a new conservation park opened up. Jesse hugged his mom. She smiled. "This is my miracle child, everyone," she said. "My husband and I were in the rainforest searching for the rare Teyano tree frog when I went into labor. I had Jesse there and when he was born, his skin was pale blue. He could barely breathe. There wasn't a hospital around for miles. There was nothing we could do. But then..." she paused and a smile came upon her face. "The very frog we had been searching for appeared along with some of its friends and covered our little boy. As they worked their magic and sang their song, Jesse's lungs started working and his skin turned pink. He was no longer blue. His life was no longer in danger. And now, as you can see, he is no longer a little boy – but my little man. He has grown so much and I am proud to say that he loves wildlife just as much as his father and I do."

Jesse nodded eagerly as his mother handed him the microphone. The bright lights and amount of people made him nervous, but he calmed himself and addressed the crowd. "Today, we are proud to announce the official opening of Granger Park. We appreciate your help and continued support in our conservation efforts. We can learn so much about each other and our world just by observing nature. If it wasn't for the observation of nature, so many wonderful things would be left undiscovered. Simple observations can lead us to a deeper understanding of nature and how creatures adapt to their environment. I like to think that we can adapt, too. I was born with a severe lung condition, yet my body adapted and I am here today. We can apply this to almost anything – our bodies grow stronger and so do our minds when we are willing to adapt. Thank you, everyone, for listening to my story. And thank you all for coming out to our grand opening and learning about wildlife with us! Please remember to respect the world around you. For tips on that, we have a booth by the north entrance."

Everyone applauded for Jesse as he handed the microphone to his father and stepped aside. Later, a few of the kids looking at a baby giraffe walked over to him.

"You're the kid that was born in the rainforest, right?" a girl asked.

He smiled proudly. "Yes I am!"

Another kid rolled his eyes. "Freak," he whispered. Jesse's heart started pounding. Did he hear that right? That kid couldn't be talking about him. Jesse wanted to brush it off, but then the kid started talking about how lame nature and wildlife conservation was. "My dad hunts all the time. Ain't nothin' wrong with it," he declared. "My mom even has a fur coat!"

Jesse shook his head and clenched his fists. He wanted to explain that wildlife offered more than trophies to mount on the wall. He wanted the others to see that conservation was more than just keeping animals around to look at them. It was about helping *living creatures* and learning from them. He also wanted to punch that kid right in the face.

Jesse had to walk away from the group before things escalated. He headed over to the aquarium where the amphibians were. Though the frogs that once saved his life weren't there, there was a similar frog that he had named Charles. He walked behind the display and gave him a few live flies. As he watched Charles eat, he said, "I promise that no matter what other people think, I will never stop doing what I can to save animals. Never. Ever."

As the frog jumped and ate the flies, Jesse could have sworn he was smiling at him. He knew in that moment that he would never give up.

Never. Ever.

Chapter Two

Emma Winstead's long hair whipped around with a strong gust of wind. She reached for her favorite lavender ribbon and tried pulling her hair back one more time; a hopeless effort. She hugged herself. She was scared. This was her first time living away from home, and so far away, too. She decided to spend the day at Granger Park. She had heard much about it and its conservation efforts. She knew parts of the park were currently open to the public for observation and she was excited to explore. She put on her favorite sundress and headed out as soon as she could. What she didn't expect was for the winds to be gusting or kick up so much dirt on her lovely dress. By the time she reached the park, though, the winds seemed to settle down. She blushed, knowing her hair must be a mess, and her clothes too, when a handsome young man approached her with a bright smile on his face.

"We don't get many visitors these days," he said, holding out his hand. "My name's Jesse. My parents own the park. What's your name?"

She took his hand, shaking it. "I'm Emma. It's nice to meet you."

"It's nice to meet you, too" he said with a smile.

She blushed and adjusted her hair. "Well, where do you suggest a visitor start?"

"How about I give you the grand tour?"

She agreed and the duo began walking. They passed by tall giraffes, ornery zebras, and majestic lions. Jesse explained not only basic facts about each creature, but each individual animal's personal story. When one of the giraffes was a baby, her mother was killed by a poacher. His parents stumbled upon her and couldn't bear to leave her in that state. She would have never made it back in the wild, so they brought her to the park. They saved her from certain death. He named her Penny.

Jesse had names for all the animals and Emma couldn't help but smile as he spouted them off. Somehow he even managed to tell the three zebras apart. She asked how and he simply responded, "I suppose it's the same way a mother can tell her identical twins apart. Besides, this one," he pointed, "has a really weird stripe on his back. See?"

She nodded and laughed. "Do you have any siblings?" Emma asked.

"Unfortunately I don't. Actually, my parents are lucky that I'm even alive."

"Why's that?"

"Oh, you haven't heard?" he laughed. "I thought everyone knew. Mom usually greets everyone that comes to the park with the full story." Jesse laughed and told the story of his birth and the frog and how ever since then he's been in love with wildlife. After he finished his story, he paused in front of the entrance to the aquarium. "Would you like to meet Charles, Jr.?" he asked with a smile.

"You're amazing," Emma blurted out, blushing.

"Thanks," he said sincerely. "Though," he continued, "I'm not sure how I earned such a response."

She laughed and then answered, while walking into the aquarium, "You just have such a passion for all this," she waved her hands at all the wildlife surrounding them. "Most people aren't even aware of anything beyond themselves. They don't see the bigger picture."

"What about you?" Jesse asked. "What do you see?"

"I see a world filled with helpless people and animals – the ones that no one else sees, because they don't benefit us. I see the fear in a cub's eyes when its mother is killed by a poacher. I see the cultures no one cares to understand. The changes in our world and the people around us. I see too much sometimes," she said. She laughed then said, "Sorry. That was a bit too deep for a simple question, huh?"

He laughed. "Not at all. I actually liked it."

She blushed again and they continued their tour of Granger Park. At the end of the tour, they ran into Jesse's parents. He introduced them to Emma and explained that she also had a passion for nature and supported the efforts the Grangers were making.

She smiled at his praises and his parents embraced her in a quick welcome hug. She had never felt such a feeling of belonging before.

Over the years, Emma continued to visit the Granger Park. She developed a close relationship with both Jesse and his family. They invited her over to many dinners. Over time, she knew she was falling in love with Jesse Granger, but she wasn't sure if he felt the same way. That was until one night after dinner at his parents' house.

Jesse took her to his father's study where there were many books about wildlife, geography, and astronomy. He pulled out his favorite book. Inside it was an essay by Charles Darwin.

"People say he's controversial," Jesse said, handing her the pages. "They judge him, but most don't even know his life story."

Emma confessed, "I don't really know his story that well myself. All I know are some of his theories and ideas."

"Did you know his wife was named Emma?," Jesse asked with a smile.

Emma blushed, but said nothing. She wasn't sure what to say. She wanted to tell Jesse that she liked him, but what if he didn't feel the same way? What then? She didn't want to be alone in this town without any friends. She didn't want to stop coming over for dinner. Not only did she love spending time with Jesse, she also loved spending time with his family. In a way, they had become her family, too.

Jesse added "She was also his cousin" and the two of them laughed for a while before Jesse looked deep into Emma's brown eyes. They sat and looked at each other, smiling, until Jesse finally said, "I really like you, you know?"

Emma's heart skipped a beat and she responded, "In what way?"

"You know..." he said, "in the I'd-like-for-you-to-be-my-girlfriend way."

She whispered, as if somehow saying it aloud would risk this beautiful moment being taken away. She was finally admitting it. "Me too."

He leaned in and gave her a quick kiss.

"I love you, Jesse Granger," she declared.

"Me too," he said, copying her earlier sentiments.

** **

After a few months went by, Emma and Jesse stood inside a small wooden church and declared their love for each other. Their vows to love each other for eternity

were met with "me too" by the other. At the end, the couple exchanged rings and kissed.

They were now man and wife. Jesse had never felt such happiness in his life. Not since the start of Granger Park. He knew that he and Emma would save many animals at the refuge. He knew they would have a wonderful life together, maybe even raise a family.

He couldn't wait to start this part of his life with the woman he loved. He knew Emma felt the same way. Though she was often quiet and reserved, he knew her soul whispered her love for him and the things he loved. It showed on the days she spent curled up with a book by the zebra exhibit and helping his parents care for the monkeys. Emma was complicated, but she was beautiful, too. He loved that about her.

Chapter Three

Jesse often wondered what it would be like to have his own family. But after their first year of marriage, it didn't seem likely that he and Emma would ever have children. He never gave up hope, though. Eventually, Emma gave birth to their first son, Jesse Jr., who they often called Junior. Being the firstborn, he gave Emma and Jesse a new purpose in life. They loved their son with their whole heart, mind, and spirit. They would have done anything for him. They were equally proud and sad when, once he turned eighteen, he declared he was leaving on an expedition. Emma was devastated but Jesse understood that this was something Junior had to do. He hugged his son, and said, "You'll be just like Charles Darwin. You'll see so much of the world. You'll learn so many things and make your own discoveries. I'm proud of you, son. Good luck."

Junior had beamed at his father's approval. After receiving a pat on the shoulder, he walked over to his mother and gave her a final hug goodbye. That was the day that has haunted Emma every day since her son left; the day she last held her baby in her arms.

Jesse Jr. never came back.

It was a rainy day when Jesse received the news. Junior's ship had gotten caught in a storm. Bits of wreckage washed up on the shore. His son had died and his body was never recovered. Jesse recalled promising his son a happy time and discoveries – perhaps even a small amount of fame, but now... now his son was gone. It

baffled him sometimes how someone who was a part of him, someone so full of life, could just be gone. Emma rarely spoke of him after his death. Any time he was mentioned, she'd leave the room in tears.

Stephen Granger was careful to avoid speaking his older brother's name. He didn't want to upset his mother. He had no intention of leaving home when he was of age. He was fine right where he was at. He loved the animal refuge. He loved wildlife as much as his father and his grandparents did.

"Mom!," Stephen yelled, "June is getting into my books again!"

"June Marie!" Emma yelled back, walking into her son's room. Sure enough there was her little toddler pulling out all the books from Stephen's shelf. "June-bug, honey, you can't do that," he mother explained affectionately.

June continued to pull out the books.

"She's gonna ruin them!" Stephen whined.

"Come on now, June," Emma swooped her up, "Let's go play outside."

Stephen breathed a sigh of relief and

began picking up his books. He couldn't believe how annoying his little sister could be sometimes, but he loved her nonetheless. She was family, and after losing his older brother, Stephen quickly learned how important family was.

Jesse Granger watched from the window as Emma took their daughter to play outside. While June played in the dirt, Emma looked longingly toward the distance, as if she somehow expected to see Junior come back home. As if she could will him back into existence.

Jesse saw this look on her face often and it broke his heart. He wanted to give her their son back, but that was impossible. For a while, Jesse stopped believing in any powers of the universe. He stopped believing in the healing powers of wildlife. He stopped telling the story of his birth. How could he share such a story when there wasn't a miracle to save his own son? He wrestled with these thoughts and these doubts every day.

That's what pained Emma the most, though – she not only lost her son, but at times, she felt as if she was losing her husband, too.

Jesse knew just what this sad moment needed, though. He called out, "Firben!" and a leopard gecko appeared at his side, a permanent smile in place. He gently petted the gecko's slick, rubbery skin and carried him outside to see June and Emma.

"Look who I brought!" he announced.

Emma smiled. June squealed at his appearance. She loved the gecko so much, but she could never quite say his name right. "F-ah-ben..."

"Yes, Firben!" Emma said, smiling. She reached over and the gecko crawled across her arm over to June. "Look June-bug, he's come to say hello."

Together, June and Firben explored the plants surrounding their home. Jesse reminded her to be gentle with them.

"Look how happy she is," Jesse said.

"She is," Emma agreed.

"F-ah-ben, let's go get some food for you."

Firben seemed to look up at her with his eyes wide, sticking out his tongue and licking his lips. Jesse laughed. "Alright, let's go get him some crickets!"

Firben loved chasing crickets almost as much as he loved eating them. He would hunt them down, corner them, and wiggle the tip of his tail before lunging at his meal. They were his favorite! Firben wasn't like other geckos, though. Not only did he eat crickets and cheer up little girls, but he also helped his friend, Jesse, on his adventures. Any time Jesse needed help, he was there. It was never a dull moment with this leopard gecko around. He had pale, yellow skin with dark spots all over, making him look just like a leopard, only he was a gecko. He was smaller and could climb into small areas in a way a real leopard could not. It was a skill that became useful to Jesse and his family, especially when June dropped one of her toys somewhere their big hands couldn't reach. Firben would quickly squeeze into the area and return the toy to the little girl. He was a valued member of the family and the Grangers loved him.

Chapter Four

Jesse loved spending time with his children, Stephen and June, but most days he was busy working as a wildlife range manager. The animals were very much like his children, and he loved them. Not only that, but the animals seemed to recognize and care for him as well.

As he opened the gate to the elephant habitat, a baby elephant named Emily came running up to him. Her mother had died while giving birth and though at first she was very sad, she seemed to find comfort in

Jesse's presence. He sat down and petted the elephant, who then climbed on top of him and nuzzled his face.

"Hello to you too, girl! I missed you. What do you say we get some food in ya?"

The elephant blinked as if to say, 'Yes, please!' He laughed and started gathering the food that the baby elephant liked to eat. She grabbed onto the food with her trunk and stuffed it into her mouth, chewing away at the delicious tree bark and leaves.

"'Atta girl!" he said, proud of the elephant. At first, she hadn't been eating. It took a long while to get her to eat from a bottle and even longer for her to eat solid foods.

After eating, the elephant ran to the pool area that Jesse was emptying and filling with fresh water. Once filled, she waded in and played in the water.

Jesse could not have been happier with his life, seeing the elephant's happiness after losing so much.

Stepping away, Jesse tended to the other animals that needed it. Firben sat on his shoulder, ready to assist in any way.

"Can you get me that eyedropper?," Jesse asked Firben, tilting his head to where his supplies were.

The leopard gecko hopped off his shoulder and ran over to Jesse's supplies, picking out the eye dropper. Last time he was given this task, he accidentally grabbed a small pen instead. He wouldn't be making the same mistake twice. Firben was quick to pick things up. He found the eyedropper and brought it straight to Jesse.

Jesse grabbed it and petted the little gecko's head. "Thank you," he said. He then filled the eye dropper with formula to feed some baby bats.

Just as he was about to start the process, Emma appeared holding June in her arms. Stephen must have been nearby.

"We have a visitor," Emma said.

"Oh?" Jesse blinked. "Well, who is it?"

"Some guy. Said he's interested in buying the refuge."

Jesse shook his head and headed outside of the nursery into the open of the park. There stood a man dressed in a fine suit, top hat, and an expensive watch.

"Hello there. The name is James Pinster," the man said. "I'd like to buy your refuge."

Jesse recognized this man. He owned the zoo across town. The animals there always looked unhappy and malnourished. Jesse had tried in vain for years to get them relocated to Granger Park. He knew this man would not care for the animals the way he did. All he could think of was the poor baby animals back at the nursery; Emily and the bats being neglected and given the bare necessities to survive. No love, no care. No – he could not sell to this man. "I appreciate your interest, sir," Jesse said, "but I am afraid I have to decline."

James laughed. "But you haven't even heard my offer! How on earth can you decline it?"

"You could offer me all the money in the world and I wouldn't be willing to sell the refuge." In that moment, Jesse could feel the truth of his words and he knew that nothing would stop him from protecting and caring for these animals.

"Oh, every man has his price," James said.

"Some things are priceless," Jesse responded.

"Well, then..." he trailed off.

Beyond the two stood Emma and June, both smiling proudly. June was holding Firben who also seemed to be smiling.

"Sir, I mean no offense, but this refuge has been part of my family since I was a child. It's in my blood, it's our home, and," Jesse paused and looked over himself, covered in grass and mud, "I don't very well see you getting your fine clothes dirty for the sake of a wild animal's happiness."

"Happiness!" the man laughed. "Animals do not experience such a complex human emotion."

"Oh, but they do!" Emma interrupted, noticing the anger rising in Jesse. "You may not believe that, sir, but they do. And we can't put a price on this refuge because, as my husband said, it's priceless to us."

"Very well then," the man said, tipping his hat and walking away in disbelief.

Jesse took a deep breath. *Why is it*

that people think only humans experience happiness and joy? As if the only creatures we can learn from are humans! Jesse shook his head and walked over to Emma and June. He gave each of them a quick hug as Firben climbed back onto his shoulder.

"I'd never give you up," Jesse whispered, petting Firben. Firben looked up with gratitude.

"Da da!" June shouted proudly.

"We're all very happy you love this place so much. I don't know what I'd do if you ever sold it! Why, I'd be stuck at home knitting or doing something boring!" said Emma.

"Me too," Jesse said, laughing.

He hugged everyone close and went back to the nursery with Firben following close behind to help. Jesse continued to care for the baby animals and then made sure the other wildlife creatures were doing well and had all they needed. He had to be careful with some of the more wild animals and respect their space. Though they could not survive on their own in the wild, it was still in their nature to be wild. They were not domesticated like Firben was. Firben never once tried to bite Jesse or his family. Instead, he was very intelligent and worked closely with Jesse. The two were as thick as thieves and Jesse was happy he found Firben and his siblings a year ago – abandoned and needing care to survive. A life without one never crossed the other's mind.

Chapter Five

A few weeks had passed since James came by to buy the refuge and Jesse was on his way to care for the animals. He thought about what life could have been like if he had agreed. It not only would have been miserable for the animals in that man's care, but for himself as well. He found joy here in nature; it was here that he could feel his happiness returning and his doubts disappear. This was his home. Besides his family, he knew nothing else but the wildlife.

As he was walking up to unlock the gate, he noticed that one of the fences was ripped wide open. The fences were so strong that not even the grown elephants could knock them down. This took effort – and human tools. Unlocking the gate in a rush, Jesse ran through the park to see what had happened. He noticed quickly that one of the animals was missing – an adult tiger. His heart sank as he noticed her absence and he wondered why anyone would do such a thing. Was the tiger simply running loose or did something worse happen? Jesse didn't want to think about it. He worked quickly to get the fence repaired, calling out for tools from Firben, who obeyed solemnly.

Emma arrived with June and Stephen. She clung tight to June and gasped. "What happened, Jesse?"

Stephen looked around with wide eyes. June started sniffling.

"I don't know. It looks like someone broke in. The tiger is missing," he explained.

Emma shook her head. "Who would do such a thing?"

"I don't know. I don't know why anyone would do something like this...whoever it was, they knew how to get the fence torn down fast. We're lucky we didn't lose any other animals."

"Is the tiger alive?" Stephen asked innocently.

Jesse walked over to his son and hugged him. "I'm not sure. I really don't know."

In that moment, Jesse realized it was hard to grieve when you had no idea what happened. He hoped they would find some answers, and soon.

He sent Emma to call the authorities and have them come by. Tears filled his eyes the moment his wife and children left. He hoped that the tiger was okay, but he had a sinking feeling in his stomach that said otherwise.

A few hours later, the police stopped by with notebooks in hand. They jotted down all the information Jesse and Emma told them.

"Do you have any known enemies, Mr. Granger?" the policeman asked ominously.

Jesse shook his head. "Not that I can think of, sir."

Emma hesitated, started to open her mouth, but shut it again. The policeman noticed Emma's movements, and asked her, "Do you have anything else you'd like to add, miss?"

"Well," Emma said, turning to her husband, "remember that man that came by wanting to buy the refuge?"

He nodded.

"What man is that?" The policeman asked the couple.

"James Pinster. He owns the zoo across town. He came by the other day and offered to buy Granger Park. I told him I wasn't going to sell but he didn't seem too upset."

Emma nodded. "But still, for this to happen so soon after he stopped by?"

"Interesting," the police man mused. "Well, thank you for all the information. I hope the fence repair comes together nicely for you. Please stay safe. We'll let you know as soon as we have any more information."

"Thank you," Emma said.

"Yes," Jesse repeated, "thank you."

After the officers left, Jesse continued to repair the fence. Little hands reached over and hugged his right leg. He looked down and saw June and Firben standing beneath him.

"Hey there, little ones," he said with a smile.

"Da da! I wanna help!"

The gecko nodded, clearly wanting to help as well.

"You do, huh?" he asked with a smile. "Well, Firben, why don't you grab June-bug a wrench?"

Firben searched Jesse's tools for a wrench that would be perfect for a toddler's grip. He came back and dropped the heavy item at June's feet. June picked up the wrench and started twisting it around the bolts on the fence, though she needed her father's help to do it. Together they put the fence back together. Emma came up with Stephen to let them know dinner was ready back home. They hopped into their vehicle and made their way back to find a nice, home cooked meal waiting for them. And a bowl of crickets for Firben.

Chapter Six

"**F**irben!" Jesse called out.

The leopard gecko came running up to him with a flashlight in his mouth. It was an early morning and Jesse was about to begin exploring the outback before the sun came up. This part of the land doubled as a conservation and breeding ground for endangered animals. It was run by the government but sometimes they needed a little help from people who actually knew about animals.

"Ah, thanks, Firben!" he said, grabbing the flashlight from his companion. "Let's go see what we can find!"

Jesse made it a regular event to search the outback. He wanted see if there were any animals in need and take notes of the animals in their natural habitat. He started walking, with Firben matching his pace, but grew tired. The leopard gecko climbed up on Jesse's back, resting his head on his shoulder.

A rustling in the trees caught his attention and he noticed several unique species of birds he hadn't seen for a while. Taking note of their behaviors, Firben wandered off. Getting lost in his research, Jesse almost didn't notice Firben running up to him with alarm in his eyes.

"What is it, boy?" he asked.

Firben lifted his head and Jesse followed the gecko into the wild. The gecko ran fast and Jesse struggled to keep up. When they finally reached their destination, Jesse felt his heart break. The carcasses of adult elephants, their tusks missing, littered the ground. There were no baby elephants in sight, which seemed odd. He instinctively

knew this was the work of poachers and anger boiled inside him. He had to do something about this.

Firben walked up to him, his usually happy smile gone, replaced by a sad look in his eyes.

"I know, little buddy. Thank you for bringing me here," he said. "We better get back home and let the authorities know what happened. And if they won't help, I'll make sure to take matters into my own hands."

Jesse doubted the authorities would do much over a case of poaching, but seeing those corpses fueled him to seek revenge. He would find a way to right this wrong – after all that nature and the wildlife of the outback had done for him, he knew that he had to do something to help.

Walking back to the refuge solemnly, Firben sat on Jesse's shoulder and nuzzled his chin. Though Firben could not speak, he did his best to comfort Jesse in this difficult time. Jesse loved the animals so much and couldn't fathom why anyone would want to hurt them, let alone kill them for profit. His heart ached and he pondered how he would break the news to Emma. Emma loved the wild as much as he did. She was currently nursing a baby kangaroo whose mother rejected it. She poured her life into their family and the refuge. To hear of such a crime, it would devastate her.

Firben nudged Jesse's chin again, bringing him back to the present. He shook off his pain and fears and knew that he would fix this – whatever it took of him, he would fix it.

As he got closer to the range, he noticed there were flashing lights and a crowd of people. *What's going on?* His heart started to pound and all he could think was that something had happened to his family. Running faster, Firben jumped off his shoulder and landed on the ground, running ahead of him. *Did someone break into the range again? Is my family okay?* He ran faster as each question plagued his mind.

Firben reached the refuge before Jesse did and found his way to a crying June. He climbed up on her just as her mother picked her up.

"Oh, Jesse!" Emma cried. "You'll never believe what happened!"

Jesse ran up and embraced his wife and children, kissing each of them on the forehead, grateful that they were alive and well. "What happened?" he asked.

"They think you did it," Emma whispered, as the police approached.

"Did what?" he asked.

"Jesse Granger?" the policeman asked.

"Yes," he said, turning away from his wife. "What's going on here?"

"We received an anonymous tip claiming that your wildlife refuge has become no more than a farm to raise and illegally trade exotic animals and that you host hunts for the highest bidders. I didn't want to believe it, but we had to come check it out. Sure enough, we found evidence of poached elephants right here in the refuge. You kept the babies alive though, it seems. Do they make you more money the bigger they get?"

"What? I would never do something like that!" Jesse yelled.

Emma shook her head, tears in her eyes. She knew the truth and she tried to tell the police officers, but Jesse quickly became their first suspect. After all, the evidence was already there.

"I swear, officer, he wouldn't do this!"

"You might be right. But we still have to take Jesse in for questioning. You understand, I'm sure."

She nodded sadly. June started crying and Stephen kept his head held low.

"Mr. Granger, please put your hands behind your back."

Jesse complied. He kissed his wife and children goodbye, put his hands behind his back, and was led by the officer to his squad car. Jesse was certain he was being set up, but why? And who would do this? It had to have been the same person who broke in the other day. Why didn't the officers consider this? Did they really think he was a criminal? He shook his head and prepared himself for the difficult times he realized were now ahead of him. Whatever was happening, he knew he'd get to the bottom of it. He'd figure out who set him up and who was poaching these innocent animals. He'd make them pay.

This was not his crime to suffer for.

Chapter Seven

Jesse found himself handcuffed and at the police station. At first, he was terrified of being alone, though he was grateful Emma was able to stay behind with the children. He didn't want her to get mixed up in this. It wasn't until he felt a little slither along his shoulder inside his shirt, causing him to jump a little, did he realize he wasn't alone. Firben had snuck along.

"Thanks, little guy," Jesse whispered.

Just then a police officer entered the room. They had been questioning him for

hours and it looked like they were back for more. *Is this what you've been doing since your parents left the range to you? Do you think this is acceptable? Your poor wife and children, what would they think of you if they knew who you really were? You claim to love animals so much, what a joke, huh?* Jesse wanted to scream at them to stop, but he knew that wouldn't help his situation any. Instead he kept repeating, "I didn't do it."

And he didn't. He could never do such a thing. Nature saved his life, he would never take a life for sport. Never. Ever.

"Jesse Granger, with this surmounting evidence, you are under arrest for the crime of funding and willingly participating in the illegal trade and poaching of animals. Anything you say can and will..."

Jesse felt as if he was drowning in the accusations being thrown at him. He only hoped that Emma knew the truth.

** **

Emma knew the truth – because she knew Jesse better than she knew herself.

"Do you think he did it?" Stephen asked.

Emma gasped. "Goodness, no! Sweetie, your father would never. I don't know who did this, but I suspect the man wanting to buy the refuge may have a part in all this. Even if your father is taken from us, James will never get this park. I won't let him"

Stephen said, "He won't love the animals like we do! Like Dad does!"

"I know," Emma said. "But you know what, whatever it takes, we'll figure this out. We won't let anything bad happen to your father or our home."

"Da da," June cried, but Stephen hugged her close.

He promised, "Daddy will be okay!"

With all of the chaos surrounding them, none of them had yet noticed that Firben was missing. Had Firben been there, he would have agreed with Emma and Stephen. Everything was going to be OK and he for one was not going to let anything happen to his best human friend.

Jesse lie on his bunk, wishing he could tuck his little June-bug into bed. He wondered if his family was alright and how long this mess was going to last. He thought about that day, many years ago, when he first met Emma. She knew how much he loved animals then, he thought, and he knew that she would know he still does. He'd never do anything to hurt any living creature without cause. He could almost hear Emma's voice whispering to him, *me too.*

In the morning, the police came to tell Jesse that he would not be let go – that even more evidence was found. The bullets extracted from the wounds of the elephants matched that of a rifle he owned.

"But..." Jesse trailed off, unsure of how to defend himself, which perhaps made him look even guiltier.

In that moment, any doubts he had about being framed washed away. He knew someone was trying to set him up. He only hoped he and his family could figure it out before it was too late.

"What do you have to say for yourself?" the officer asked.

Jesse remained silent. There was

nothing he could say.

Later that day, Jesse managed to obtain paper and a pen from another inmate and wrote a quick note to his family. "Firben," he said, "I need you to go back home and give this note to Emma. And stay there! It's not safe for you here. I'll miss you, little buddy, but you gotta go back. Look after June-bug and keep her safe."

Firben seemed to nod and took the note in his mouth, nuzzled Jesse's chin, then ran away. Firben always ran fast but this time, he ran faster than ever before. He knew this note was important. Although Jesse asked him not to return, Firben would not let his friend suffer. He'd figure something out to save him when the time came, he just knew it!

****

Firben arrived at the range with the note in hand, or rather in mouth, and walked up to Emma – a sad smile on his face.

"Firben!" she declared. "We've been

looking all over for you!"

"F-ah-ben!" June squealed, and ran to her gecko friend. She picked him up gently and held him up to her in a hug.

Emma took the note from Firben's mouth and began reading.

Dearest Emma,

It pains me to say that I will not be coming home soon. They have matched the bullet from the elephants with the rifle in our house. The one my father passed down to me from his father. It appears that I am being set up. I'm not sure why. Stay safe, please. Keep a close eye on the children and don't let them wander too far. Look after the refuge while I'm gone. Don't let anyone hurt any more of our precious animals. I will come home... as soon as I can find a way out of this mess.

Stay safe, my love.

Yours always,
Jesse

Emma had tears in her eyes, but they were tears of hope. Something in her told her that this would all work out. She spent her next days drowned in the activity of caring for the animals at the refuge. June and Stephen helping her each step of the way – Firben too. Everyone took charge of caring for the range while Jesse was in jail.

Though she didn't think it would be wise to risk sending him a letter back, every night she vowed to do as he requested, because she knew that one day he would return.

Chapter Eight

As the evidence continued to mount up against Jesse Granger, he was informed he would soon be going to trial. Each piece of evidence that came in only made Jesse look guiltier than he had days before. In handcuffs and a jumpsuit, Jesse was led to the courtroom. There were two things in this dark time that brought him joy - he was going to see his family today and he would finally be able tell the world his story. A story he had long since stopped telling after his son's death.

It pained him that the entire town believed he was guilty. His good name was now stained by a terrible lie, but at least his family knew the truth.

Not only does Jesse see his family at the trial, but he notices the man who tried to buy the refuge is there. Could he be the one who framed him? Jesse wasn't sure, but he looked directly at the man who didn't even flinch.

Taking a seat at the stand, Jesse was asked if he swore to tell the truth. He said yes and was then asked a series of questions about his ownership of Granger Park.

"Have you ever poached any animals?" the town's lawyers asked.

"No."

"Do you know or associate with anyone who poaches animals?"

"No."

"Is it not true that you've had animals missing from the park – one you even reported?"

"No. I mean, yes it's true."

"Did you cause that animal to go

'missing'?"

"No," Jesse said, breathless. His anger was reaching through him and he wanted to scream *I am innocent.*

"Can you explain how the bullet found in the elephant matches rounds fired from your rifle, Mr. Granger?"

"No, I cannot."

The defense came to the stand and started asking Jesse a series of questions as well.

"There were fourteen animals missing as follows: an elephant, red panda, a crocodile, skink, lion and tiger cub, grizzly bear cub, snake, panda, penguin, sea turtle from the saltwater tank, gorilla, pangolin, and rhino. All babies. All missing."

Jesse grew sad and sighed as the memories of his times with each animal listed flooded his mind. "Logan...Cameron ..."

"What's that?"

"The lion and the tiger cub," he said gently. "They were best friends, sir."

"Do you have names for all your animals?"

Tears in his eyes, he said, "Yes."

"Can you tell me their names?" the lawyer asked.

Nodding, he said, "Dakota the bear cub. Emily the elephant. Flaker...she was the baby penguin. Then there was Kai the sea turtle."

"And that," his lawyer turned to the jury, "is evidence that my client could have never harmed these innocent animals. Can you not see the pain in his eyes? He loves this park as much as he loves his own family. He would never hurt his own family." The lawyer waved his hand in the general direction where Emma, June, and Stephen sat close together. Firben peeked through June's jacket, showing his support and love as well. "So, why on earth would he harm those animals? There is no evidence of any profit here. It is clear my client has been framed. Please, do not punish an innocent man for a crime he did not commit."

Interrupting, Jesse said, "I know I'm not supposed to interrupt or say anything more, but your honor, I was raised to love animals from the day I was born. When I was born, I almost died, but this tree frog that the natives of the rainforest thought had healing powers, well, it hopped on me and I was healed. I was near death, but I came back, and my parents vowed, as did I, to always look after nature and keep the wildlife safe. Sometimes I may doubt the power of that tree frog, but I will never doubt my love for wildlife. Please, believe me when I say, I would never harm another living creature. Not for money. Not for anything. It is not in my character to do so. Whatever you believe about me, please realize that isn't me."

Emma smiled brightly at her husband, proud of his courage. People began to shout. The jury seemed shocked and the judge called for order in his courtroom.

"Please, everyone. Let us break for recess while the jurors makes their decision."

Jesse's lawyer promised they'd created enough doubt to keep him from being sentenced, but as time dragged on for the jury to make their choice, Jesse wasn't so sure. Emma and his children came by to visit him with Firben in tow. He hugged each of them.

"I am so sorry," he whispered.

"You did nothing wrong," Emma declared.

"Nevertheless, I put us at risk. I should have been more cautious with who I let come near the park."

"You trust people. You see the best in everyone, Jesse. It's not a bad thing."

"I saw that man who tried to buy the refuge in the courtroom today. James."

"So did I. Do you think he's the one that framed you?" Emma asked.

"I didn't at first but it seems that way. I think so, anyway."

"But dad," Stephen asked, "why would someone do this to us?"

June stayed quiet, a sad look in her eyes. Firben cuddled with her, but nothing seemed to help cheer her up with her father gone.

"I don't know, son. Maybe for money. Maybe out of spite. Either way we can't lose hope! They might still let me go. We'll figure this out."

After the recess, Jesse was informed that the jury had come to a decision. He said goodbye to his family as he was escorted back to the courtroom, Firben hiding in his shirt again.

Chapter Nine

"We the jury have agreed and come to the conclusion that Jesse Granger is guilty of funding and willingly participating in the poaching of wildlife animals including exotic and endangered species," a female juror stated.

Jesse hung his head low.

The judge nodded and said, "Animal trafficking is not a victimless crime. When you participate in the illegal trade of animals and animal products, you aren't just gaining an exotic pet or buying trinkets. You're supporting a criminal underworld. Not only are innocent animals abused and killed, but whole ecosystems can be thrown off balance. Crime rates rise and communities become increasingly dangerous as the lust for money causes poachers to employ bolder tactics. Animals aren't the only ones that suffer. People suffer, too. Due to the scale and severity of Jesse Granger's crimes it is in our best interest that he should be executed. Therefore, the execution date it set for July 5th. I will give you time to make your peace, sir. Please make your final arrangements and say your goodbyes, Mr. Granger."

Jesse had no words in that moment and he didn't dare look toward his family. He felt Firben in his shirt once more, sliding his little face along his shoulder, as if to say – it will be okay. Jesse knew it would, but he wasn't sure how. He knew he couldn't lose hope, though. He wanted to shout at the jurors – could they not see that he was innocent? Were they not concerned about sentencing an innocent man to death? But

the evidence against him would sway anyone to believe he was guilty, and so it was.
He forgave the jurors for he knew that he
too would have made the same choice had
he been in their shoes.

Taking a deep breath, Jesse stood after everyone in the court was released. He
wanted to say goodbye to his family, but he
would rather wait until it was closer to his
execution date. Instead, he gave them each
a nod and a smile, as if to say he'd figure
it out. Perhaps he could appeal? Perhaps
someone with new information would come
forward in time for him to avoid the execution. He could only hope.

For the next few hours, Jesse spent
his time in his cell analyzing everything that
had happened in the past few weeks. He
knew he was being framed. If he could just
figure out who was pulling the strings, he'd
be able to set things straight. He wished his
family well and hoped that they were not too
troubled for his sake. He never wanted to
cause anyone pain; humans or animals.

His cellmate across the way shouted,
"What did a decent guy like you do to end

up in place like this?"

Jesse sighed. He almost ignored the man but he didn't want to be rude. "I'm accused of poaching and pretty much ruining the world, but I didn't do it."

"That's what they all say." The man laughed. "And I don't think you had anything to do with ruining the world. It was like this when we got here."

Jesse shook his head. "I suppose so."

"Well, for what it's worth, I'm sure you're innocent. You look the type."

Despite himself, Jesse laughed. "At least someone thinks so. I was sentenced today."

"Oh yeah?"

"To be executed," he continued solemnly.

"You're kidding me? All over a bunch of animals?"

"They're so much more than that!" Jesse stood tall, waving his hands. "I don't know why anyone would do such a thing. They're not all so different from us, you know?"

The man nodded, but Jesse could tell

he didn't understand nor care.

"Well," the man said quietly, "I hope they find out you're innocent."

"Me too," Jesse whispered, thinking of his dear Emma. "Me too."

Meanwhile, at the Granger household, Emma and the kids had begun making a board filled with all the potential suspects who might be framing Jesse. Emma believed wholeheartedly that it was James, but she had no proof. Jesse's lawyers insisted that with no proof, she seemed like a desperate wife longing to have her husband back home. Though she agreed she was desperate, there was something off about that guy and it haunted her mind.

She wondered – having lost most of her hope – what might happen to her, the children, and the refuge should Jesse not find freedom. Would she be able to care for all of the animals on her own? Would someone like James come and try to take away the refuge from her? Or would the courts take it away because of Jesse's alleged crimes? Her heart broke thinking about it but just as she was about to cry, little June walked up and gave her mother a hug. "It'll be okay," she sang.

"Aw, June-bug, you're right. I know you are!" She smiled.

"She sure is!" Stephen declared.

Together the family worked toward finding an answer for Jesse. They had little time, but they knew they had to do something. They were set to meet with him in a few days and they hoped they would have good news for him by then.

Both Jesse and Emma spent the following days trying to figure out who might be behind this. Jesse bounced ideas off of his cellmate who was soon to be released. His cellmate promised he'd look into what he could, but Jesse knew the man probably had no intention of helping him once he was out. Nevertheless, he smiled and thanked the man whose name he found out was Tim.

"I think you're right. That guy wanted to buy your refuge for a reason. This all started right after he came along, right? Why didn't the police follow up with that?"

Jesse answered, "They did, but there was no evidence linking him to the crimes.

I'm the one whose rifle shells were at the crime scene."

"Man, you're being framed big time!"

Tim grew up very differently from Jesse. His father was a musician and left him alone with his little brothers while he went on tour. It wasn't a glamorous life and it led to many of his reckless behaviors. Jesse pitied the man, but he seemed to have an insight into criminal minds that Jesse didn't.

"That man probably wants to do the same thing you're being accused for. Perfect crime, really."

Jesse sighed. "Perfect crime, but why?"

Tim answered, "Because he can. It's that simple."

But for Jesse, it was never that simple. Not only was his mind haunted by leaving his family behind, but he was also haunted by his dear friends, the animals, at the refuge. Firben had been going back and forth between the home and jail, bringing Jesse letters and sending letters for him. Emma swore the animals were doing fine but he wasn't there for them and wondered if they missed him. He knew he would meet with Emma and his family tomorrow, just a few days before the execution was set and all he could think was: How does one say goodbye forever?

His hope was wearing thin.

Chapter Ten

Jesse woke up in the morning to meet with his family. They were tearful but resigned to his fate. Their lack of hope pained him.

"I tried everything, Jesse. We looked everywhere. We can't find any evidence..." Emma said apologetically.

He pulled her close, kissed her forehead, and said, "It's okay. I know you did your best." He stopped and looked at his two children. "All of you."

For a moment he wondered if he'd

finally be seeing his oldest son again – in another life far different from this one.

Emma seemed to have read his mind and offered a gentle smile and a kiss on the cheek. "It'll all work out one way or another, my love. If not now, in another time."

He kissed his family farewell. Firben too. It was time he went somewhere safe, lest he be caught in Jesse's cell. Jesse could only what they'd do to the little gecko if he was caught with him.

Later the next day, a few of Jesse's friends stopped by. He was relieved to see them, but his relief quickly turned into sadness.

"How could you do this?" one of his friends asked. "There isn't enough money in the world worth the pain you're putting your family through. Never mind those poor animals!"

Jesse tried to argue his innocence, but their minds were made up.

"I didn't do it," he pleaded.

"Oh save that for a fool! Your wife might believe you but I don't. Shame on you, Jesse Granger. Look what you've done to your family name!"

"I've done nothing!" he declared, but the more he fought the more the other man seemed convinced he was guilty.

Another friend came in, tears in her eyes. He went to hug her, he wanted to say goodbye, but the friend simply shouted "I thought you were better than that. How could you lie to us? How could you do that?"

Worn down from the previous visits, Jesse said, "Is there any way I can prove to you I didn't do what they say I did?"

His friend simply shook her head and left.

Why didn't anyone believe him? Jesse wondered broken-heartedly. The words of his friends were just as hurtful as that day when the refuge first opened and the kids teased him for loving animals. Now his friends hated him for allegedly hurting animals.

All he could think, the only thought that consoled him, was *I know I didn't do it. I know I am good. The animals know I didn't do it. Firben knows. Emma knows. My whole family knows. That is all that matters.*

Though that may have been all that mattered, the courts still continued with plans for his execution – and the day had finally come.

"We'll be taking you to the center of the town," an officer explained.

Jesse simply nodded and silently followed the man. Once outside the building, Jesse was forced to walk through the town. People stood by, shouting curses and calling him a poacher and a killer. Tears filled his eyes but he held his head high. He would not act guilty. He was not guilty!

They reached the middle of town and there sat a stand of sorts with a few steps. Jesse was led up the steps and to the center of the gallows. A noose was placed around his neck. He was to be hung publically. He scanned the mob until he found Emma.

She squeezed her children close to her but stayed standing still.

"Final words, sir?" The judge asked, standing calmly in such a frightening place.

"Yes," Jesse said, his hands bound and his voice scratchy from the noose putting pressure on his neck. "I don't know who framed me or who the real poacher is but I know it isn't me. I may be the only one who knows that, but I assure you – death will not stop me from finding out who this poacher is. Whether in this life or the next, you must pay for your crimes. You *will* pay. Justice will be sought for the lives of those animals."

A few people in the crowd snickered. The judge visibly rolled his eyes. "Very well then," he said. "Anything else you want to add?"

Jesse looked over to his wife and children. "I love all of you so much." Tears filled his eyes.

Emma mouthed, "Me too."

Jesse smiled gently, remembering the many times they had said those same words to each other. When they fell in love, when they got married, and throughout their married life together. *Me too.* Jesse continued his speech, looking directly at Emma, "I will never stop looking after you. I will be in the wind, the eyes of a newborn tiger, the waters of the ocean...I will be with you all until you are with me. I love you,

Stephen. Stay strong for your mother and sister. June-bug, you are a beautiful girl. Don't ever stop loving animals the way you do. Look after Firben – he will be your best friend and he will look after you, too. I wish it didn't come to this. I wish we had found out the truth, but alas, this is my fate. Remember, I am always with you. Until we meet again."

Emma nodded solemnly, tears in her eyes. She only wished she could have found out who really did this. She took a deep breath and prepared herself for the worst. She wanted to close her eyes, but they stayed glued to Jesse's eyes; her love and her life.

Shielding her children's eyes, she prepared for the rope to tighten and her world to leave her.

What she didn't notice was that Firben had slipped off her shoulder. Neither her nor Jesse had any clue what was about to happen, but while he was making his speech and saying his final goodbyes, Firben had a plan.

Chapter Eleven

Right before Jesse had started his speech, Firben crawled gently off of Emma's shoulder and toward Jesse. He snuck through the crowd, running so quickly, that even if anyone looked at him, all they would see was a blur running past them. He was so quick and stealthy that Jesse didn't even feel him crawl up him.

Firben knew that Jesse was innocent. He had no doubt in his mind and he set to work nibbling on the rope holding his friend captive. It took him a bit longer than he anticipated. After all, he had been eating mostly crickets these last few months. But his teeth were still strong. He nibbled and nibbled and paused only for the briefest second, when Jesse mentioned his name. Should his plan fail, Firben knew he must look after June – and the rest of the family! The speech went on and with each word, Firben chewed more.

"Alright then, let's get on with it!" the judge declared. As the executioner went to pull the lever and release Jesse Granger from this world for a crime he did not commit, Firben chewed through the last thread. Jesse dropped, the rope snapped, and he hit the ground with a loud thump. His heart filled with joy as he realized he was alive. Firben crawled upon his shoulder with a smile on his face. But the reunion didn't last long.

Chaos erupted. Jesse looked up to see his family running towards him waving their arms frantically. The judge and other authorities followed close behind. Emma got to him first and quickly untied his hands before giving him a kiss. As the executioner closed in, a figure came out of nowhere and tackled him to the ground. It was Jesse's old friend, Tim.

"Run! You have to leave!" Emma shouted.

"It's the only way, Dad!" Stephen pleaded.

"Run!" June-bug declared.

Jesse was reluctant to heed their advice but he knew if he didn't move quickly, he'd be facing death once more. So Jesse ran. He ran faster than Firben ever did. Faster than any person he ever saw. He didn't know where the strength or the speed came from, but he was grateful for it. Perhaps it was a gift from the frog that day, a gift to live no matter what. Jesse knew he could have died the day he was born, but somehow he lived, just as he could have died today, but here he was – running for his life.

At first, Jesse didn't know where to go, so his legs carried him to the only place he knew. The refuge. He knew it was probably the first place they'd go to look for him but he had to get his gear.

He kept expecting to see the authorities following him but he was too fast for them to keep up. Their shadows were nowhere in sight. The only person beside Jesse was Firben, running fast and doing his best to keep pace.

"Oh," Jesse said as he got a leg cramp. He sat down for a moment, expecting the authorities to finally catch up, but they didn't.

Firben walked up and nuzzled his leg, as if to say, *we must keep going.*

Jesse stood up, tall and strong, and began the trek once more. Though his pace did slow a bit, he got to the refuge faster than he ever had from town.

He paused as he saw the gates, his heart pounding. Suddenly, he heard shouting behind him. The authorities had caught up with him.

"No!" he muttered to Firben. "Let's go. I need to get my supply bag. Then we can get out of here."

Firben nodded. Jesse scooped him up and put him in his shirt pocket. "Best keep you safe, little buddy!"

With that, Jesse ran over to the gates, hopped the fences, and ran.

Chapter Twelve

Jesse knew the refuge better than anyone. Not only did he work there, but he grew up there. He knew the ins and outs, all the hiding places and how to slip out without going through the main exits. Firben bounced in his shirt pocket as he ran to the tiny office of his. It was not that long ago he was caring for the baby animals. Maintaining the refuge. He missed it, but he couldn't think about that now. As he ran, he passed by many of the animals. He wanted to stop and say goodbye to each of them, but time and circumstance would not allow it. Instead, once he got to the nursery, he began unlocking a case that contained a bag he kept for emergencies. It contained a tent, non-perishable food items, medical supplies, and other items that would hold him over until he could find his own refuge from the authorities.

Throwing the pack around his shoulder, Jesse could hear footsteps outside. Quiet as a mouse he slid over to the opposite end of the building and exited. Firben kept an eye out as well and would nudge Jesse anytime he noticed one of the men approaching.

With each twist and turn, Jesse slipped through trees, cracks in the fences, and even walked amongst the lions who were familiar enough with him to not hurt him. He would escape this. He knew it. He wanted to say goodbye to his family one more time or bring them along with him, but he knew that would be too dangerous. He had to get out of the refuge now and lose the authorities following him. He knew it was just a few more turns until he reached the exit. An exit only he and Emma knew about. He had snuck out to meet her through it many times when they were younger. *Oh,* he thought, *those were the days. Simple and sweet. What has life become?*

Whatever his path was now, he knew he should be grateful that he was alive. He gave Firben a quick kiss on the forehead. "Thank you," he whispered, as they slipped out of sight from the refuge and the police looking for them. Jesse petted the little gecko and quietly stalked out into the wild.

He smiled. *I was born in the wild. It won't hurt me to live in it for a while.*

He waited until he was far away enough from the refuge to be sure that no one was following him or able to track him down. He pulled out the tent from his supply bag, and began setting it up. It took him and Firben a few hours before they were able to get the tent set up comfortably, but they managed. Setting up tents was not in either Jesse nor Firben's special skills.

Once the tent was set up, Jesse realized how famished he was. He rummaged through the supply pack and pulled out a glass canning jar his wife had used to store preserves and other items. He began nibbling on the preserves and a few crackers.

He offered some to Firben, but the gecko licked his lips and began searching for his own food. Food wasn't hard to come by for a gecko out in the wild. After a little bit of hunting, he returned to the campsite with a full belly and a smile on his face.

"What are we gonna do?" Jesse asked. He had gotten away and he found a safe place, but he wasn't sure what to do beyond that. Oh, he knew he wanted to find the man that set him up, but how? How was he going to accomplish this? Firben didn't have any answers.

What Firben did have though was the rifle casing the police had found that linked Jesse to the crime. He dropped it at Jesse's feet. Jesse picked it up and shook his head. Anger filled his chest and he looked up to the sky, the wildlife and nature surrounding him. He said, "I vow to find the man that hurt these animals and destroyed my life. Whatever it takes. He will pay."

Jesse knew that even though he didn't know how to find that man yet or how he'd stay hidden long enough to, he knew that he would. He knew that he would stop this criminal and get his life back. He hoped and prayed that Emma and the kids knew that as well – that one day he would be back to care for them and the refuge. He sent out his promise to God, the universe, whoever would listen. Firben crawled up beside him, ready to take a nap. Jesse couldn't sleep, though. His mind was reeling with adrenaline from his near-death experience. Instead, he grabbed his journal. It was the only non-survival supply he brought with him, but he knew it would come in handy.

He sat down at the edge of the tent with his companion on his shoulder, pulled out a pen, and began writing.

** **

While Jesse wrote, his family sat crying at home. They looked everywhere for Firben, but of course, they could not find him. June cried for both of them. Her mother assured her that Daddy would come back and Firben, too.

Stephen didn't believe her, though. Stephen hoped she was wrong because he was afraid that if his father ever came back, he would die. He couldn't bear the thought of that. Instead, he made his own vow to the world – he would care for his family and look after the refuge, just like his dad did when he was young. He would make sure June-bug was safe and his mom, too.

Still, he lied to June-bug just like his mother did. "Daddy will be back," he promised. The lie tasted bitter on his tongue, but it made June stop crying.

That night, Emma wrote a letter to her husband, though she thought he would never get the chance to read it. She didn't even know if he'd survive out in the wild, but she wished with her whole heart that he would.

He wrote until the sun went down and Firben was fast asleep. Closing the notebook, he knew he finally had a plan.

The poacher who ruined his life would be found, and he would pay dearly for his crimes. Jesse would make sure of it.

One day, Jesse vowed silently, not only would the poacher pay for his crimes, but Jesse himself would be reunited with his family. He hoped it was before his children were too much older. He had already lost one child to death, he was not going to lose his other children. No matter what it took, he'd hug Emma again one day and kiss her cheek. He'd teach Stephen how to feed and care for the baby elephants, and he'd help June-Bug with her homework. He'd be their father again. He needed that.

And he knew that just as the frogs had once helped him live, so would nature, whether it was Firben or another creature, help him to get back to his family and his home. That was all that truly mattered. The truth, his freedom, and his family – which included the animals at Granger Park. He wondered what his parents would think of him if they were still alive. He knew they would be proud of him. Despite the trials and the accusations he faced, Jesse never fully lost hope. Here he was, fighting for the truth and for the wildlife – the wildlife that had saved his life on so many different occasions. If it wasn't for the refuge he would have never met Emma, or had his children Jesse Jr., Stephen, and June. He would never have had any of these experiences and memories that he cherished so dearly.

He fell asleep with these thoughts, cuddling Firben to keep the gecko warm during the night.

When he woke up there was a small breakfast of fruit beside him, gathered by Firben.

"Thanks, little buddy!" he said. Picking up a berry and popping it in his mouth, Jesse declared with a smile, "Let's go find that poacher."

Jesse Granger will return...

LEOPARD GECKO

Class: Reptile

Origin: Southern Asia, Pakistan

Size: Up to ten inches but some have grown to a foot long!

Family: Gekkonidae

Status: Not endangered

Appearance: Most are yellow with black spots all like a (really small and rubbery) leopard.

Leopard geckos store fat in their tails and can access it when they've gone without food or water for a while.

They are carnivorous and stalk their prey.

Unlike most geckos, they have eyelids for blinking and closing their eyes when they sleep (but can still lick their eyeballs clean when they feel like it).

They also have little claws instead of sticky pads like other geckos.

They will lose their tails if they feel threatened so handle with care!

Their tail will grow back but it won't look as nice as the original.

They are nocturnal which means they like to party at night and sleep all day (sort of).

ABOUT THE AUTHOR

Jeston Texeira is a former student of Texas A&M University and a volunteer at the Cameron Park Zoo in Waco, TX. His biggest literary accomplishment so far is winning an area-wide writing competition when he was in 4th grade. Other accomplishments include getting a job right out of college and at one point being the youngest candidate in Texas to run for state representative at the age of 22. Born in Hawaii and raised in Texas, Jeston grew up admiring Steve Irwin and Bear Grylls for their love of wildlife and sense of adventure. His passion for educating children and helping animals is what led to him devoting his free time to volunteering at the zoo where he gets to do both! He hopes to one day work at the Australia Zoo with Steve Irwin's family. His other heroes include Ernest Hemingway, Chris Kyle, and Donald Trump. Jeston lives in College Station, TX with his leopard gecko, Firben. This is his first book.

Made in the USA
Middletown, DE
21 September 2021